4. The Netherlands

The Netherlands is as flat as a pancake. It is full of black-and-white cows, thousands of windmills, and millions of tulips. It is not true that everyone here wears wooden shoes; only the fashion-conscious do.

5. Italy

Spaghetti, vermicelli, bigoli, linguini, capellini, bucatini, perciatelli, tagliatelle, fettuccini, pappardelle, penne, rigatoni, farfalle, fusilli, ditalini, and maccheroni are all different names for the same thing—pasta, Italy's favorite food and ours too—yum!

6. Spain

Spain is a country full of color: red oranges, black bulls, green olives, and yellow-sand beaches. Spanish people love flamenco, a style of dance and music that originated in southern Spain. It is sometimes confused with the flamingo, a large, pink, silly bird with an upside-down beak.

12 Papua New Guinea

Australia 11

New Zealand

10

10. New Zealand

For some reason, someone in New Zealand decided to name their national bird and their national fruit the same thing—Kiwi. It is true that they do look alike. Kiwis (the birds) can't fly because they never have enemies to escape from. Kiwis (the fruit) are flown all over the world, where they end up in fruit salad. Sheep outnumber people in New Zealand twenty to one, and have the right of way on all the roads.

11. Australia

Australia is the smallest continent in the world, and one of the least populated per square mile. The population of 178 million includes 136 million sheep, 24 million cows, and 18 million people. The people live mostly on the edges of the country because the center is hot, dry, and miserable.

12. Papua New Guinea

Papua New Guinea is the home of the world's largest butterfly, Queen Alexandra's birdwing, with a wingspan of up to 12 inches. Even though only 4 million people live here, they speak more than 700 different languages.

For Kenneth and Eugene

Illustrations copyright © 2005 by Milton Glaser

Text copyright © 2005 by Shirley Glaser

Deep thanks to Deborah Adler for her endless
ethusiasm and for making this race get off
the ground.

Printed in Hong Kong
First Edition
1 3 5 7 9 10 8 6 4 2
Reinforced binding
Library of Congress Cataloging-in-Publication Data
on file.
ISBN: 0-7868-1821-2
Visit www.hyperionbooksforchildren.com

The Big Race

PICTURES BY MILTON GLASER WORDS BY SHIRLEY GLASER

Hyperion Books for Children   New York

Tommy Tortoise was waiting for Harry Hare in front of the 42nd Street Library in New York City. "Let's have another race," Harry said. "Okay, but just remember, I won the last one," said Tommy.

Turn Over Here

The windstorm turned into a tornado and swept Harry high into the air. He looked down, saw the finish line, and thought, I've won the race! Wait a minute: is that Tommy already there?

Harry took off like a shot, shouting, "I'm out of here!"
"Shouldn't we say one, two, three, go?" Tommy asked.

In a matter of moments, Harry had left Tommy far behind. In fact, he was already in France. He could see some farmers carrying their cows.

Harry knew he was back in the USA, because he saw a half dozen grizzly bears taking steam baths in Yellowstone Park. He also could see that a windstorm was starting up.

The next time Harry
looked up, he checked
Big Ben, England's most
famous clock. He was
making very good time.

"I don't know how long
I was asleep, but
anyhow, here I am in the
Dominican Republic
and I don't have far to
go. With Tommy's tiny
feet, he has to be
miles behind me."

Harry came upon fields
of beautiful red tulips as
far as the eye could see,
and knew he was passing
through the Netherlands.

When he arrived at the
Galápagos Islands, Harry
needed a little nap.
While he was sleeping,
something passed him by,
much to the amusement
of a blue-footed booby
standing nearby. A bit
later, the booby's laugh
woke Harry up.

He was moving faster than the wind as he zipped by a building that looked as though it were about to fall over. None of the Italians walking nearby seemed worried about it.

Harry ran carefully
through a forest of
Mexican cacti. He was
beginning to feel a
little sleepy.

Harry's nose was twitching. The aromas of garlic, olive oil, and oranges, and the sound of guitars made him realize that he was in Spain.

It was much warmer in Hawaii. Harry was happy to get past a giant volcano that was rumbling and smoking and seemed about to erupt.

The snowstorm finally
ended. A Royal Canadian
Mountie helped Harry by
pointing out the direction
to Hawaii, where the
weather might be better.

It was getting hot and
very dry, but Harry kept
going. In the distance, he
could see the pyramids
and a caravan of camels.
"This must be Egypt,"
he said to himself.

Harry moved on and
suddenly came upon
hundreds of Brazilians in
bathing suits dancing the
samba on a long stretch
of beautiful beach.

A cold, blinding snow-
storm in Russia slowed
Harry down for a while,
but he kept going.

A touch of frost on his nose told Harry he was passing through Antarctica. A family of penguins was ice-skating and sliding down hills of snow.

Harry came to an unusual building, known as the Parthenon, on top of a hill in Greece. Even though it was very old and broken down, Harry thought it was one of the most beautiful buildings he had ever seen.

The miles were whizzing
by. Harry was surprised
to come upon a painted
cow wearing a garland of
flowers. If I were a cow,
Harry thought, I'd like to
live in India.

There were so many
sheep walking on the
road in New Zealand that
Harry could hardly see
which way he was going.

When Harry saw
dozens of kangaroos
jumping over one
another, he assumed that
he was in Australia.

By the time Harry got to China, the sky was filled with dragons, fish, and butterflies. Chinese people fly their favorite kites when they feel like celebrating something.

In Papua New Guinea, Harry saw two men on stilts who were fishing in the middle of a lake. The houses nearby were also on stilts, as was a very big sign.

With the wind whistling by, Harry passed Mount Fuji, shining brightly through the clouds, a favorite subject of Japanese woodcut artists for hundreds of years. He was sure that he was way ahead of Tommy Tortoise in the big race.

Turn Over Here

13. Japan

Japan is made up of four large islands and four thousand small ones. Japanese people love Mount Fuji, raw fish and rice (sushi), green tea, and cherry blossoms. As soon as the first blossoms appear in the spring, thousands of families flock to the parks to have picnics under the flowering trees.

14. China

China is really big, with more people living there than anywhere else. A thousand years ago, the Chinese people built the longest wall in the world. Fortunately, it is wide enough for ten people to walk side by side. It would take six months for you to walk from one end to the other, so bring sandwiches.

15. India

India is full of bright, beautiful colors. Indian dyes are made mostly from plants like crocus, indigo, madder, pomegranate, lac, walnut, tea, and katchu, and are used to color everything from textiles and food to cosmetics and paint.

19. Hawaii

Hawaiian shirts are known all over the world, although the native Hawaiins prefer to call them aloha shirts. Aloha means "greeting," "hello," and "farewell." The bold, colorful designs are based on native plants. Aloha shirts are worn big and loose, which makes them perfect for a hot day. The average year-round temperature of Hawaii is a balmy 70 degrees. Aloha.

20. Mexico

For children's parties in Mexico, the children make a clay or papier-mâché animal filled with candy, fruit, toys, and other surprises. It is called a piñata. The piñata is hung from the center of a room, where the children whack it as hard as they can with a stick. Everything falls out, and all the children share the treasures. You may want to make one for your next birthday.

21. The Galápagos Islands

The Galápagos are nineteen islands named after the giant tortoise. The islands are full of marvelous birds and animals, many of which cannot be found anywhere else on earth. One such creature is the blue-footed booby, a bird that incubates its egg by standing on it, instead of sitting on the egg, the way all other birds do.